HELEN HANCOCKS

PENGUIN
IN PERIL

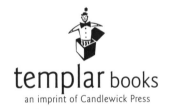

templar books
an imprint of Candlewick Press

One afternoon, three hungry cats ran out of food.

They searched the house high and low
and found three gold coins.

They set off for the grocery store.

On their way, the cats passed a movie theater.

A movie called *The Fishy Feast* was playing.
They handed over the three gold coins and went in.

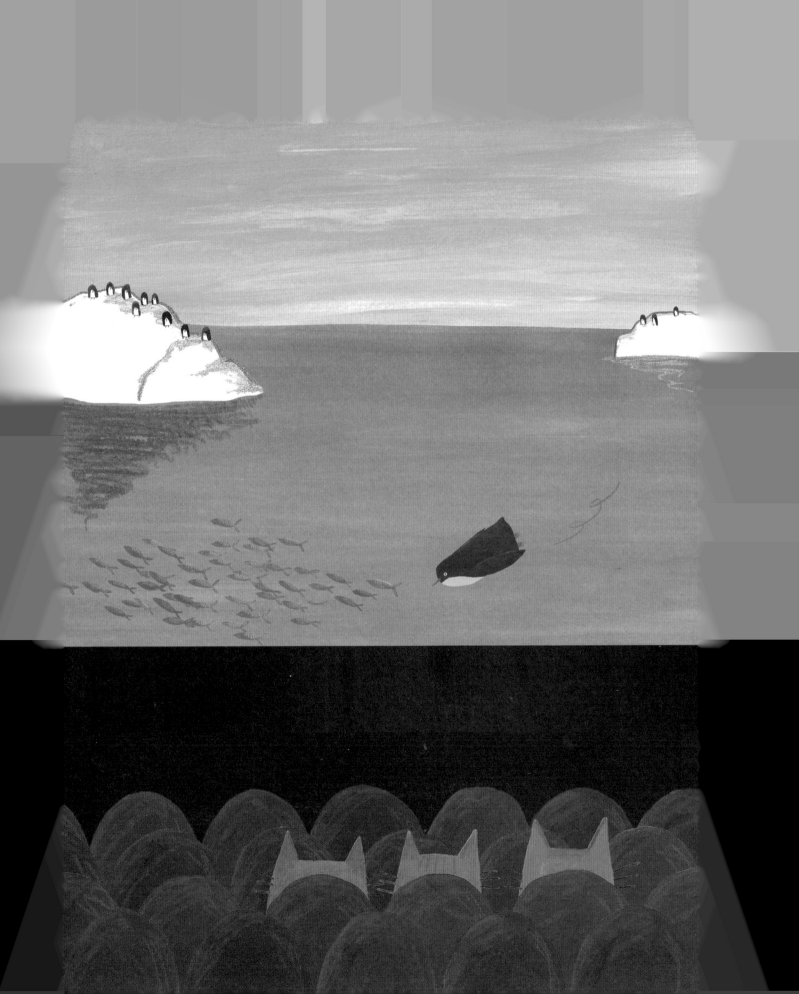

NOW SHOWING

THE FISHY FEAST

12:00   3:20   6:40   8:10

Later that evening,
the cats emerged from the movie.

They had food on their minds
more than ever . . .

but the movie had given them
a brilliant idea.

Around the kitchen table, they formed a cunning plan.
It would be the most brilliant robbery of all time.

Soon they would have their own fishy feast!

All they needed was . . .

a penguin.

One dark night, they put their cunning plan into action.

They entered the zoo
with an empty sack . . .

and left with a penguin.

Back home, the cats tried to tell the penguin
the next step in their plan.

They didn't speak Penguin very well . . .

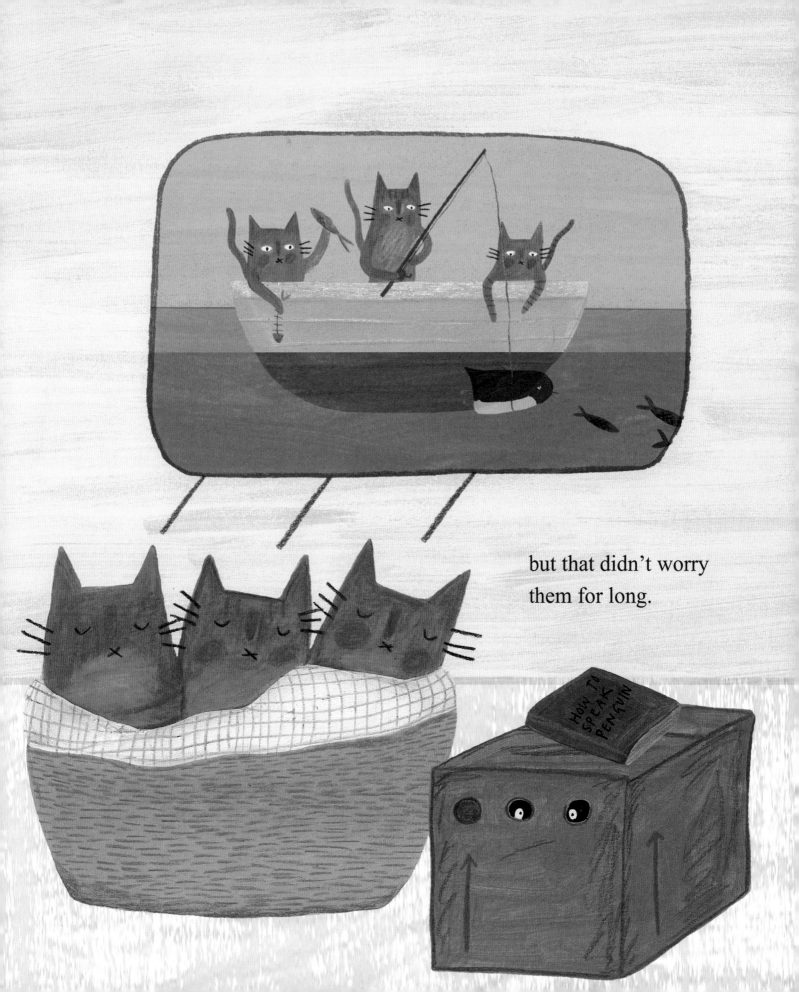

but that didn't worry them for long.

The next day, they set off on the fishing trip.

The penguin began
to sense that he was in peril.

Anxious to get home, he
made a break for freedom.

The cats ran after him . . .

but the penguin proved quite difficult to spot.

They almost caught him
on the subway.

They almost caught him in a restaurant.

But the penguin was always one step ahead.

A little bird spotted the penguin
in peril. The penguin told her
that he wanted to go home.

Luckily, she knew a secret way
into the zoo.

While the cats chased
after the penguin . . .
the little bird had a word
with a friendly police officer.

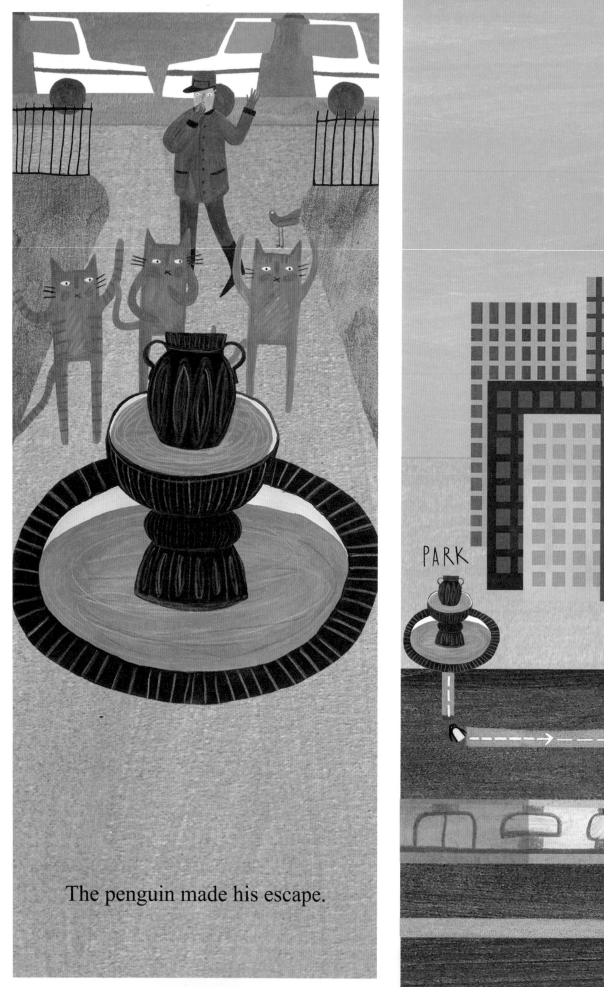

The penguin made his escape.

PARK

ZOO

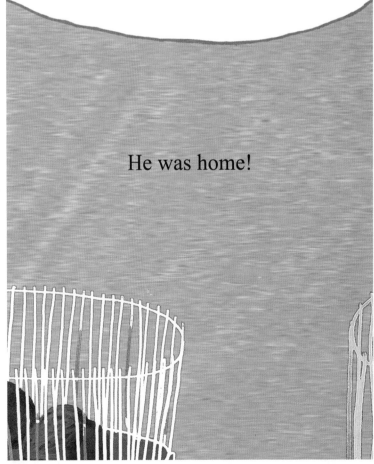

He was home!

Just in time for a fishy feast!

And as for the cats . . .

DAILY NEWS

CAT GANG FOILED

CATS GET GRUEL FOR LIFE

CUNNING PLAN FOILED - PENGUIN NOT HARMED.
CATS RECEIVE GRUEL FOR LIFE AFTER KIDNAPPING
A PENGUIN FOR BIG FISH CARTEL.
THE PENGUIN WAS FOUND BACK AT THE ZOO
UNHARMED BUT HUNGRY FOR HIS FISH SUPPER.

For my mum xx.
And thank you to K
and L, R, F, E, I, J, T, and D
for putting up with me.

Copyright © 2012 by Helen Hancocks

First U.S. edition 2014

Library of Congress Catalog Card Number 2013943078
ISBN 978-0-7636-7159-4

13 14 15 16 17 18 TLF 10 9 8 7 6 5 4 3 2 1

Printed in Dongguan, Guangdong, China

This book was typeset in Times New Roman.
The illustrations were done in mixed media.

Edited by Jenny Broom
Designed by Mike Jolley

TEMPLAR BOOKS

an imprint of Candlewick Press
99 Dover Street
Somerville, Massachusetts 02144
www.candlewick.com